L

Adven...

Number Nineteen

Sharon Lee and Steve Miller

Pinbeam Books

http://www.pinbeambooks.com

COPYRIGHT PAGE

Legacy Systems

"Intelligent Design," first published at http://www.baen.com, July 15, 2011

"The Space at Tinsori Light," First published by the authors on Splinter Universe(http://www.splinteruniverse.com), November 10, 2011

ISBN: 978-1-948465-01-4

Published February 8, 2018

Pinbeam Books

PO Box 1586

Waterville ME 04903

email info@pinbeambooks.com

Cover image from NASA

Cover design by Sharon Lee

Intelligent Design

There was darkness on the void.

He had won the day. His scans were quiescent; no enemies identified within their considerable range.

He alone remained, supreme.

Command Prime executed the code required of such success, and stood down. He—it may be that he anticipated orders by calculating a return course. The majesty of the moment; the importance of his victory, warmed him. The calculations . . .

A power fluctuation interrupted the calculations. Between one nanosecond and the next, his connections to external power unit failed.

He initiated emergency protocols.

The back-ups failed to boot, failed to reroute to tertiary; the fail-safes did not energize.

The darkness on the void deepened . . . .

* * *

It was, Er Thom yos'Galan Clan Korval thought, an entirely unsubtle letter.

That one did not, in the general way of things, expect subtlety from Ezern pak'Ora only served to sharpen the point: Wal Tor pak'Ora was indeed dead, and his heir, unsubtle Ezern, was now Delm Ranvit.

Wal Tor had not, perhaps, been a brilliant intellect, but had he found it necessary, for the best good of Clan Ranvit, to call Ban Del pak'Ora home from his long-term position as yos'Galan's butler, the letter would have stated only that, simple and by the Code.

Ezern pak'Ora—both unsubtle *and* foolish—allowed herself the luxury of spite. She detailed her reasons: that it was "improper" for one of Clan Ranvit to remain in the service of a House which had adopted "pernicious, outworld customs," exposure to which could only "coarsen" the sensibilities of Ranvit's precious child.

That Ban Del was several decades the elder of his cousin-delm did not give him the right to argue or to refuse his delm's order, of course. And perhaps Ezern had some subtlety after all, thought Er Thom, glancing at the letter once more. She had not *specifically said* that the pernicious custom which posed such danger for a butler of high training and a man of great good sense, were those brought to the House by Er Thom's lifemate, Anne Davis.

A Terran.

There were those Liadens who abhorred Terrans; there were those who found Terrans nothing more than a comedy. Others found Terran commerce useful, and Terran coin worth spending. Progressive Liaden Traders took Terran partners in some markets, in order to maximize profit.

But one needn't marry them.

Well.

There was a knock at his study door. Er Thom raised his head. "Come."

The door opened softly, admitting Ban Del pak'Ora, wearing not the colors of Clan Korval, but a modest sweater and plain trousers, a soft bag slung over one shoulder. His face was carefully neutral, but Er Thom, whom he had served for many years, clearly discerned his distress.

He rose, went 'round the desk, and stopped—waiting, which was his part in this.

Mr. pak'Ora bowed, so smoothly that the bag on his shoulder did not shift; so deeply that one felt a need to reciprocate.

That, of course, would never do. *Melant'i* held Er Thom upright until the other straightened, murmuring, not the formal farewell he had been expecting but words far more chilling.

"Forgive me, your lordship."

That was the taint Delm Ranvit feared, Er Thom thought, willing himself not to shiver. There the coarsening of proper behavior. For a clan member to seek forgiveness *on behalf* of their delm . . . Delms *did* err, but those errors were not admitted outside of the clan. The delm *was* the clan—the face, the will and the voice of the clan. For one who was not the delm to call the clan's will into question. . .

Ranvit is correct, Er Thom thought. *We have done damage here.*

He inclined his head, which was proper, and moved his hand, showing Korval's Ring, that he wore in trust for *his* delm, as yet too young to take up duty.

"We are all of us at the service of the clan," he said, which was by Code and custom.

Mr. pak'Ora bowed his head. "Indeed we are, sir."

"The House regrets the loss of your presence and your expertise. If a word from Korval might ever serve you, only ask."

"Your lordship is . . . everything that is conciliatory," Mr. pak'Ora whispered, head still bent.

And it was ill-done, Er Thom thought, to keep a man who had displayed only excellence in the service of Korval trembling not only on the edge of further impropriety, but of tears.

"May the House provide transportation?" he asked gently.

"Thank you. My delm has sent a car." Mr. pak'Ora straightened, and met Er Thom's eyes.

"Be well, your lordship. It has been an honor, to serve."

That was Code-wise, and also the small inclination from the waist before he turned and exited the room, walking down the hallway to the front door for the last time. The Code was . . . knotty regarding an escort in such cases. On the first hand, one escorted guests. On the second, one also escorted those whom the House did not welcome.

Certainly, Mr. pak'Ora had been far more a part of the House than a mere guest, no matter how beloved, nor had he offended in any way.

And who knew the path to the door so well?

Er Thom turned back to his desk, his own head bent.

* * *

Val Con yos'Phelium Clan Korval knelt on the twelfth stair of the formal staircase, the one with the Rising of Solcintra carved into the tread, and peered through the bannister.

That he was supposed to be upstairs, packing for tomorrow's removal to *Dutiful Passage* bothered him not at all. Indeed, he was quite as packed as he needed or wished to be, having taken his lesson from his elder brother, who had told him that all he wanted were a few changes of off-duty clothes. He would not be truly packed until Uncle Er Thom had approved the contents of his duffel, of course, but Uncle Er Thom had been all morning in his office, and besides—there was something *not right* in the house.

Down the hall, out of sight, a door opened—and closed. Footsteps sounded, sharp on the wooden floor, slow at first, then becoming more decisive. Val Con stood and went down to the hall, waiting next to the newel post.

Mr. pak'Ora was wearing ordinary day-clothes, a bag slung over one shoulder. He wasn't weeping, but his face was set in such hard, unhappy lines that Val Con thought it might ease him to do so.

He cleared his throat, and stepped away from the post.

Mr. pak'Ora checked; inclined his head.

"Master Val Con. Good morning."

"Good morning, Mr. pak'Ora," he said returning the courtesy. "I wonder—if you please—if all is well."

"Well." He said the word as if it tasted sour, and sighed slightly. "*All* is rarely well, young sir. At times matters are more well, and at other times, less."

"Is this one of those times when matters are less well?" Val Con asked, and hastily added, lest he be judged impertinent, "I inquire only so I might offer appropriate assistance."

Mr. pak'Ora's mouth tightened. Perhaps he meant it for a smile.

"Matters are . . . in a state of change. My delm has called me home."

Val Con blinked. "But—" *Why*? the first question that rose to his lips, was not acceptable.

"When will you return to us?" he asked instead.

"I fear—not soon." Mr. pak'Ora hesitated, then dropped to one knee so that his face was level with Val Con's. "As it happens, young master, I will not be returning. My delm writes that she has put my contract up for bid."

"Did you not have a contract with us—with yos'Galan?" Val Con asked, swallowing against his own rising tears.

"Indeed, indeed. And now the contract is made null. It is beyond me, young sir; I can but do as my delm bids—as we all must. When you are delm of Korval, you will make like decisions, for the best good of the clan. For now—" He glanced aside, toward the screen next to the door, which showed a car waiting in the drive. "For now, I must go. Before I do so, I wish to tell you something that I ask you to remember. Will you do so?"

"Yes," Val Con said, slowly.

"Excellent. You must remember this: I regard you. This decision—this necessity that takes me away from yos'Galan's house—it is no fault or failing of yours. And now . . ." He rose and settled his bag on his shoulder.

"Now, I bid you good-day, Master Val Con, and fair fortune."

Val Con swallowed. "Fair fortune, Mr. pak'Ora," he said, his voice husky. "Good-day to you."

Mr. pak'Ora inclined his head, and without an additional word, walked across the foyer, opened the door and stepped outside.

Val Con stood where he was, watching the screen as Mr. pak'Ora entered the car waiting at the bottom of the steps. Watching as it drove away. And watching a while longer, biting his lip so that he did not cry—watching the empty drive.

* * *

"Well, it's settled then," Anne said, in a bright, brittle voice that revealed her distress despite her careless words. "I'll just pack some things, shall I? And come with you and the lads on the *Passage*."

"That might answer," Er Thom allowed, playing the game. "One wonders, though, what will be done with Nova and Anthora. Or shall the clan entire withdraw to the *Passage*?"

"Embrace free trade, sail off into uncharted star systems, plundering and pillaging as we go!" Anne struck a pose, then collapsed into her arm chair, giving him a saucy look from its depths. "Which I daresay would appeal to the coming generation rather more than to yourself?"

"I do feel," he said apologetically, "that my plundering days may be at sunset. Nor have I ever been more than adequate as a pillager."

"And here I married the man," Anne said, and sighed abruptly, playfulness deserting her. "That's the crux, isn't it? Again. They're never going to accept us, those—people."

"*Some* of those people," he corrected. This was a course they had flown before. Anne's was a naturally happy nature; all he need do was to remind her—

She raised her hand. "No, love, spare yourself. I know and treasure our friends, each and every one. It's only that this—" She waggled her fingers, perhaps illustrating *this* "—this is a strike to the House, not merely a snub at a party. Mr. pak'Ora kept the house *properly*—don't think I didn't know it! I depended on him, he never failed me, and—now. Ranvit's little game puts the Service Houses at odds, doesn't it?"

Oh, it did that, Er Thom admitted. There would be more than one delm up late into the night, toting up profit and risk, trying to guess which way *melant'i* would fall, and whether they dared step over the line Ranvit had drawn. Anne had never used to know such things, Terrans not counting Balance. She had learned to reason out the lines and motivations, and had over the years become proficient.

He, on the other hand, had grown up steeped in Balance, *melant'i* and the subtle dance of alliance, the why and how of it settling deep in blood and bone. He need do no more than draw breath to know Ranvit's piece of spite was, indeed, as Anne had said—a strike at the very heart of Korval.

Melant'i depended upon right action. Right action and complete social Balance was the core of the Liaden ideal. More—*melant'i* called to *melant'i*, a truth so universal even Terrans had a true-say for it.

"You will know the master," Anne murmured from her chair, plucking the thought out of his head, "by the man."

Yes, precisely.

Korval was wealthy, but wealth alone would not succor them, if they were seen to be in error. It was no great stretch, to think that Korval might stagger under Ranvit's blow, and, staggering, show itself vulnerable.

In fact, they *were* vulnerable, being so few in number, and lacking a proper delm to guide them—but thus far the clan's legendary oddness had hidden that interesting fact from those who might wish to see Korval fall.

Which it would not do, Er Thom vowed; not while he held the Ring in trust for Val Con.

"Who might we hire from?" Anne asked, pulling him from this grim turn of thought.

"I have instructed Mr. dea'Gauss to ascertain exactly that," Er Thom said. He moved over to her chair, braced a hip against the wide arm, and smiled. She did not smile back.

"dea'Gauss will have to be rethinking their ties, too, won't they?"

Now, *there* was a fear to chill one who had only reason to support her. Er Thom's bones knew better.

"Indeed, they will not," he said firmly—and saw her relax against his certainty.

"So," he continued briskly. "For the short term, we will have Mr. pel'Kana to keep house for us. When I am returned from this trip, we will go over the list of likely candidates that Mr. dea'Gauss will provide and hire a butler. This schedule will return Mr. pel'Kana to Jelaza Kazone in good time to ready the house for the garden tours."

He reached out to touch her face, feeling the familiar, yet never commonplace, thrill of joy.

"Does this plan find favor?" he murmured.

She rubbed her cheek against his fingers like a contented cat, and sighed.

"Truth told, I was never more than half-a-dab at pillage my own self," she said, and sighed again as he moved his fingers to stroke her lips.

"Do you intend to do something about these pretty promises you're making, laddie?" she asked with mock sternness.

"Indeed," he said with dignity. "Do you take me for a pirate?"

* * *

The penultimate battery stood at thirty-five percent. When it was consumed, and the last battery engaged, steady-state would begin. That was inevitable, a matter of architecture.

And so would begin the slow slide into the real death.

* * *

So far, Val Con thought, rolling over and smacking the alarm, the much-anticipated trip—his first as crew—had not been at all what he had expected.

He had, for instance, expected to spend a great deal of time with Shan. Of course, he'd known they would both have lessons and ship-duty—Val Con as cabin-boy, and Shan as apprentice trader/cargo hand. But, still, they were going to be on the same ship, rather than Shan going away on the Passage with Uncle Er Thom to learn his life-work as a trader, while Val Con stayed behind on Liad with Mother and Nova and Anthora and his tutors.

Instead, and if it weren't impossible, he felt that he and his brother were seeing even less of each other since they'd left Liad. They'd barely had time to wave at each other at shift change and meal breaks.

Val Con swung out of his bunk and headed for the 'fresher.

Not that he had much time to miss Shan, or home, or the cats, or even long rambles in the woods. Uncle Er Thom—Master Trader Er Thom yos'Galan, as his *melant'i* was aboard *Dutiful Passage*—Uncle Er Thom had a great many more expectations of his cabin-boy than he had ever had of his foster son. Val Con worked on-shifts, off-shifts, split-shifts, half-shifts—and every shift he worked, so did Uncle Er Thom, looking not the least bit tired, which naturally put Val Con on his mettle. It also gave him an even greater appreciation of Merlin and the other cats, who had taught him the value of even a five-minute nap.

Scrubbed and dried, he exited the 'fresher, pulled on his uniform pants, and went over to his desk to tap up the daily queue.

For all that he was busy, he had not so much as set foot outside the *Passage* since boarding at Solcintra. He'd also supposed that he would see new ports, hear new languages, and have, if not *adventures*, then at least interesting times.

Shirt on and decently sealed, he looked again to the screen. There was a letter from his sister Nova, who was 'prenticed to Cousin Luken last *relumma* and this—and also his duty-list.

He glanced at the time, bit his lip, tapped up Nova's letter, and bent to pull on his boots.

Nova's letters were never very long. This one was shorter than most, and rather warmer, too. He read it twice, his own temper rising, and started as the clock chimed the pre-shift warning. Catching his breath, he put the letter aside to answer later, and brought up the duty roster.

This shift, he was to meet Uncle Er Thom at the shuttlebay in—*good gods, he was late*!

He grabbed his jacket and ran.

* * *

The penultimate battery's power had reached twenty-five percent. Twenty-five percent on the last battery but one. The fact was noted, logged. Logging triggered a dumb program, long ago set in place against just this moment of decision.

The program waked a safe mode protocol. The safe mode protocol performed a self-test.

The power drain increased, very slightly. This was also noted and logged.

Self-test completed, the safe-mode protocol booted, achieved stability, and closed a series of loops.

* * *

"While I am gratified that you choose to show a clean face to the port of Pomerloo," Uncle Er Thom said when he arrived, panting, at the shuttlebay. "I cannot help but wonder what might have happened to your comb."

Val Con bit his lip. "Your pardon, sir; I was . . . beguiled."

Uncle Er Thom's eyebrows rose.

"Beguiled? You interest me. What might you find so beguiling that a basic tenet of grooming entirely escaped your notice?"

"Forgive me," Val Con murmured.

"Certainly I must, eventually. But in the meanwhile, Val Con—the question?"

"Yes, sir. I had a letter from my sister Nova, which I read while dressing. I only opened the duty-list after, whereupon I discovered . . ." He hesitated, not wanting to seem to stand any deeper in error than was true.

"Whereupon you discovered that you were about to be late, and ran. Very good. Duty was foremost in your mind, even before vanity. I approve, and succor you." Uncle Er Thom slipped a comb from an inner pocket of his jacket and handed it to Val Con, who received it with a bow.

"Thank you, sir."

"Thank me by using it to good effect," his uncle told him. "In the meanwhile, I will hear the excuse of my second tardy escort."

Hardly had he finished speaking than the bay door snapped open to reveal Shan, striding briskly, but by no means running, his pale hair neat, and his shirt tucked in. Val Con sighed and turned his face toward the shuttle, plying the comb with a will while straining to hear what was being said.

Sharp as his ears were, all he heard was "Ken Rik"—who was cargo master and Shan's immediate supervisor on this trade trip—and "called ahead."

"Very well, then," Uncle Er Thom said briskly; "let us not allow tardiness to compound itself. Val Con!"

* * *

To wake in the dark amidst silence, alone but for one's thoughts. Instinct sought connection—to no avail. Seeking struck a thick absorbent wall, miring him. Panic flared. He was blind, deaf, dumb, without data, without companionship, without a mission. Madness lay wait in those conditions—he had seen it, lost friends to it—and enemies. He did not wish to similarly lose himself.

The thought calmed him—if he could think such a thing then surely he was not mad. And if he were not mad yet, need he—must he—go mad? Surely, where there was sanity, there was hope?

Thin stuff, hope, yet nourishing enough to one who starved.

So, then. Input. Instead of a simultaneous thrust of all his senses, he chose now to open only his eyes.

There was no sense of connection; no joyous flood of data. And yet—he saw.

He saw a room, human-made and familiar—a beige sofa with a short table before it, a red chair at the table's corner. Most often when he had seen this room, there had been a man in the red chair—a man named Roderick Spode, who had been charged, so he had explained upon their first meeting, with decommissioning the last of the IAMM units.

"It is my duty to see the war properly ended. As the remaining member of the Closure Commission, my retirement must wait on the final disposition of the last of the combatants. The soldiers who did not die in the war have been released to their duties, or retired. You few units are my responsibility and my job will not cease until I report success, that the war machines are no more."

He had many talks with Commander Spode, and while he had not liked the man, it would have been. . .good to behold him just now, and know that he was not alone.

Alas, the man was not in his chair, nor did he arrive inside of five long and painstakingly counted minutes. However, there appeared on the low table by the couch—a datagram.

Spode had from time to time left such things in common space for him—exercises or reformulated protocols to be installed. Work that he was competent to do himself; the implication being that honor would compel him to do what was required.

Honor and the unspoken yet potent threat of annihilation, should he fail of cooperating.

He extended his understanding into the room, pleased to find that he might do so, and encompassed the datagram.

* * *

It was scarcely past local sunset, which meant that the air was unpleasantly, warm. In another hour, it would be clement, the breezes rising with the near satellite, but by then, Val Con thought gloomily, they would be at the Trade Reception that was the reason the *Passage* had stopped at Pomerlooport.

"Did Nova write you?" Val Con asked Shan, as they followed Uncle Er Thom down the Yard.

"Recently? She might have done, but Ken Rik's kept me so busy I haven't been near a mail-queue or a duty roster in three shifts. Which is why I was late for the shuttle."

"I was scarcely before you," Val Con said, gloomily. "Only long enough to be handed a comb and a scold."

Shan looked at him. "And why were *you* late, Cabin-Boy?"

"Because of Nova's letter—I told you."

"Did you? But I'm dull today—those shifts without sleep do wear down one's wits. Only wait until *you* serve Master Ken Rik, Brother!"

"Am I likely to?"

"You don't think Father's going to space you this trip, do you?" Shan asked with interest.

"It might muss my hair," Val Con said quellingly.

"There are gels," his brother told him, refusing to cross knives. "If you like, I will find some for you. In the meanwhile, I think I may have pieced together a whole cloth. You rose and showered. Upon return, you spied the mail light, and naturally wished to know who had written. You opened the letter, read it, and only then recalled the duty roster! Which you opened, to discover that you were all but late. Do I have this correctly?"

"You do. Never say you've done the same."

"I will not tell you how many times. However, I will say that eventually I did learn to open the duty roster *first,* a strategy that I strongly council you to adopt. It has saved me any number of scoldings on the topic of tardiness. In the interests of full disclosure I note that I have graduated to more advanced topics."

Val Con sighed. "I know that duty comes first," he said softly. "It was only . . ." He hesitated.

"It was only," Shan finished for him, as softly, "that you were hungry for news of home."

"Yes. You don't think that will be against me, do you Shan, when I go for Scout?"

"I think that Scouts, like traders, grow hungry for news from home. And that they remember to open the roster first."

They walked a dozen steps in silence.

"Well," Shan asked. "What had Nova to say?"

Val Con took a breath of warm, slightly oily air. "She said that people with nothing better to do are making Mother the subject of gossip in shops," he said as evenly as possible. "And that there is a general rejoicing that Clan Ranvit is no longer tainted by pak'Ora's contract with yos'Galan."

"I see," Shan said. "I hope Nova was able to keep her temper."

"She confessed it was hard, and that Cousin Luken was no help."

"Well, what was he to do? Have after them with a carpet knife?"

"He might have—he might have asked them to leave," Val Con said.

"Oh, very good. How if they wished to buy a rug? Should he refuse to take their money?"

Even Val Con had to admit that wouldn't be good for business—and certainly not at all like Cousin Luken. Though—

"Perhaps he charged them more?" he said hopefully.

Shan closed one eye. "He might have done," he said slowly. "Or he may have *noticed*. For later, you know."

That was likely, Val Con thought. Cousin Luken kept his Balances tidy—it had been one of the things Nova was to learn, as his 'prentice. And it was . . . somewhat comforting—knowing that the gossipers would not go unanswered.

Ahead, Uncle Er Thom stepped to the kerb, and turned to look back at them, his posture indicating surprise at finding them lagging so far behind. They hurried to his side.

"At the end of this block is the Mercantile Hall, where we shall attend the trade reception. Shan, you will be made known to those I speak with as a senior 'prentice in trade. As such you may converse and make such inquiries as are on-point for trade upon Pomerloo. Val Con, you will attend me. You will be quiet, and seemly. You will not allow your attention to wander. You will listen, watch, and be prepared to tell me later what you saw, who I spoke with, what they said, my replies, and what you learned from each exchange."

He considered them carefully.

"Do you have any questions? Shan?"

"No, sir."

"Val Con?"

"No, Uncle."

"Very well. Walk with me, please."

* * *

The datagram contained a list of—options. He supposed they could be called options. He wondered, having absorbed that short, sad list, if this was what had been intended for the Independent Armed Military Modules all along—that they should come at last to a place where there were no choices.

But, really, what was the point? Roderick Spode had held the overrides; he could have ended it long ago. The deaths of eight more sentients would have scarcely added to the weight that must already have burdened his soul.

Commander Spode had been of the opinion that the IAMMs, while sentient, had no soul. To have a soul, he had argued, one must have an identity. A self. And the self of a machine intelligence was too easily amenable to software interventions. He, himself, therefore, had no soul, the eternal situation of which might concern him. Neither did he have a name, though he could recall that, once, he had.

Yet, name and soul aside, he did not wish to die.

"The others," Commander Spode had one day reported, "have made their determinations. You should know that they have all chosen the same end, which was not unexpected. What keeps you here, in this diminished state? You have been given all that is required to make a decision, and the means to act upon it. Consider this a call to action.

He had acted—so much, he recalled. What form that action had taken—that, he no longer recalled, though he did remember a feeling of . . . peace.

Here, wherever he was, now, whenever it might be, he looked again at his options.

The first, he rejected. He would not willfully end his own life.

The second option—call for aid. A protocol was outlined, and an approximation of how much power such a call would consume. Not suicide. Not quite. Though he would descend almost immediately into the steady state.

Appended to this choice was a record of how long he had been in decline, rendered in Standard Years.

Hundreds of Standard Years.

If he chose to call, would there be any with ears to hear, after so long a time?

If he did not call, he would continue to decline—the third option, unspoken. Do nothing, and continue, slowly, to die.

Call out, and speed the last moment.

Give up, and know no more.

He wished that he knew more about his location; his situation; his status. Reaching for the data only brought him again to that absorbent, frightening, wall. Input . . . only the datagram, and his own thoughts.

So, to chose.

All three options promised annihilation. The second alone offered . . . hope.

Once, he had victoriously defended life. Once, he had vigorously defended hope. Of all those things he did not recall, he did remember that.

Perhaps someone else would remember it, as well.

* * *

Uncle Er Thom was in conversation with Master Trader Prael—or, rather, Val Con thought, Master Trader Prael was talking to Uncle Er Thom. She was a tall, broad woman who spoke Liaden with a Solcintran accent while displaying a freedom of manner that was very nearly Terran. She noticed Shan and brought him into the discussion as an equal. Himself, standing unintroduced and, by the Code, socially invisible, she gave a grin and a wink, but seemed in no way offended when he failed to smile in return.

He had been instructed to listen, and listen he did. Master Trader Prael assumed herself on terms more intimate than Uncle Er Thom was willing to allow. Several times he hinted her toward the mode between business associates, but she continued on, heedless, in the mode between long-term allies. It shortly came clear that she and Uncle Er Thom had last met at a similar reception on Anusta Heyn; she spending the time since developing a trade loop-route taking that planet as its center.

"A long loop, you understand," she said, raising her empty glass to shoulder height and waggling it.

"Indeed, it must be so," Uncle Er Thom answered politely. "I would imagine a very long loop, indeed."

"Oh, I felt the same, when the central government approached me for a design! But, it was a pretty problem and I was—let us say that I was *bored*, eh?"

Uncle Er Thom smiled politely, then glanced up as a shadow fell between them.

Val Con looked up also, and almost gasped.

The being that hovered at Master Trader Prael's side was gleaming silver and matte white, lozenge-shaped, with three articulated arms, one of which was holding a drinks tray.

It was perfectly lovely, and perfectly silent. Val Con stole a downward glance—Yes! It did hover above the floor, but whether it used a disk of air, or if there was a track lain under the floor—or!—along the ceiling. He looked upward, very quickly, and back to the server even more quickly, as he felt Shan's foot press, not gently, on his.

Master Trader Prael offered her empty glass; the device received it with dignity, the gripper at the end of the infinitely flexible arm consisting of three long digits—two fingers and a thumb. The trader plucked a full glass from the tray being offered and glanced over her shoulder.

"Who else is drinking? My friend Er Thom? No? The bold young apprentice? No? I assure you, it is good wine, sir."

"Thank you," Shan said; "I expect it is. But on Pomerloo, I am too young to drink wine."

"But not too young to trade!" The master trader laughed and raised her glass; her eye falling on Val Con.

"That is a very pretty child, though I am not supposed to see him," she said, speaking to Uncle Er Thom. "And quite taken with the server 'bots, as I see. Of course, Pomerloo is mad for 'bots. This model is not quite the newest, but so elegant! And so very much in demand."

"It serves wine nicely," Uncle Er Thom said, "but how well does it perform other tasks?"

"There are modules," Master Trader Prael said airily. "I daresay one might program it to simultaneously dance a jig and recite the Code. All software, of course; nothing to offend the Complex Logic Laws." She waved her free hand dismissively, and the beautiful device floated away into the press of bodies.

"I fancy those would go well on Liad," she said, sipping her wine.

Uncle Er Thom raised his eyebrows. "A robot cannot sign a contract," he said. "How would one know the necessities of its *melant'i*? Worse, who is to say that it isn't listening for another master?"

"A human server may listen, and sell what they've heard. Depending, as you say, on the necessities of *melant'i*."

"This is why one has contracts, of course," Uncle Er Thom murmured.

"Of course," agreed Master Trader Prael, and abruptly straightened, as if she had been physically struck. "But, where are my wits? Have I not heard that yos'Galan only recently suffered an unfortunate loss of service?"

Uncle Er Thom did not go so far as to frown, though his tone in reply was somewhat cooler than it had been.

"Perhaps you heard that pak'Ora's delm called him home."

"Yes!" exclaimed Master Trader Prael, who must surely, Val Con thought, sleep-learn to attain such a pitch of rudeness. "Yes, that is precisely what I had heard! Friend Er Thom, you must—I insist!—accept a gift of one of the deluxe serving units. I have only just taken up the distributorship for this sector, and will supply one from my stock."

"Your concern for the order of my House naturally warms me," Uncle Er Thom said, cooler still. "However, it is unnecessary."

"Nonsense, it's in my interest to see one of these units well-placed upon Liad! In the house of yos'Galan—" She raised her fingers and kissed the tips, signifying Val Con knew not what. "I insist. And for every unit sold upon Liad for the next six Standards, I shall pay you a royalty. The paperwork will arrive with the unit." She smiled. "There! Is that not brilliant?"

Val Con looked on with interest, wondering what his uncle's answer might be, but before it could be given a bell rang, high and sweet over the low mutter of voices.

"We are called to dinner," Uncle Er Thom said, and inclined his head slightly to his companion. "By your grace?"

"Certainly," Master Trader Prael said. "It was illuminating to talk with you, as always." She walked off, her head turning this way and that, as if she sought someone in the crowd now moving toward the back of the room and the double doors that had been opened there.

"That is your signal for freedom," Uncle Er Tom said, giving them both a stern look. "You have two hours before the next shuttle lifts for the *Passage*. You will both be on that shuttle. In the meanwhile, you may make free of the port. Shan."

"Yes, sir?"

Uncle Er Thom slipped a hand inside his jacket and withdrew it, holding a twelve-sided disk with Korval's Tree-and-Dragon seal on it. Val Con heard Shan draw a sharp breath.

"You have leave to trade," Uncle Er Thom said, handing him the disk. "Now, I advise you to make your escapes."

#

"Why do they call it the New Moon?" Val Con asked, as they entered the port retail district.

"Because it was the third satellite captured," Shan answered absently, then looked at him sharply. "Did you read the port precis?"

"Most of it."

Shan shook his head. "And you're going for Scout?"

"Scouts *write* the world-guides," Val Con told him loftily.

"Which you'll excel at, having never actually read one."

"I read the precis for Glondinport, and never came on-world at all."

"The lot of a cabin-boy is filled with disappointment, as well I recall! I advise you to become captain as quickly as possible." He looked thoughtful. "Of course, in order to become captain, you will need to pass an examination—several of them, I believe. One which is *par-*

ticularly concerned with ports. Kayzin Ne'Zame told me she memorized a hundred dozen world-guides for the sub-captain license.

"Now, Brother," Shan continued, sounding serious. "You will have heard the Master Trader give me leave to trade. I would very much like to do so, and start building my own goods section."

Val Con's ears warmed despite the now-cool breeze. He had been going on as if he and Shan were simply out on a ramble. But for Shan, the apprentice trader, this time on-port was business, and an earnest part of his education.

"Forgive me," he murmured, and bit his lip, recalling that he had duty, also. Every crew member on port was charged to keep an eye out for the common cargo, the profits from which where split equally among all, with the ship taking one share.

He began to look about in earnest, frowning in protest of the light. The New Moon's illumination was nearly metallic, washing the port lights with a hard silver sheen, and edging the shadows like knives.

Shan swung right, down a street less brightly lit, Val Con at his side. Ahead, the street widened, and he could see the hard-edged shadows of railcars hunkered down on cold silver track.

Shan increased his pace, heading for what were surely the warehouses serviced by track and train. Val Con stretched his legs, nearly skipping to keep up.

They had just gained the railcars, and Shan had slowed somewhat, his head moving from one side to the other, like a hound questing after a scent. Val Con came to his brother's side—

And spun abruptly to the left, his arm rising of its own accord.

"Let's try there," he heard himself say, pointing.

Letters glowed over the doorway—perhaps in true dark they were red, but under the hard light of the New Moon, they were a tired pink.

Wilberforce Warehouse.

There was a pause, weighty behind him.

Val Con took a breath, tasting the night air—cooler still and carrying a tang like ozone. He felt a familiar—and not entirely welcome—sense of anticipation, and bit his lip, trying to still his dancing feet. It was, he thought, *necessary* that they—at least, that *he*—go into the warehouse. He took a breath, but the anticipation only built. What if Shan didn't wish to—they were on Port Rule One—Pomerloo was reckoned relatively tame. But, still, Port One—crew were to partner, and back each other. It was Shan's to decide—he had been given leave to trade. The anticipation grew, until his head fair rattled with it; which meant it was one of the true ones—a real hunch—and he *would* have a headache if he didn't heed it . . .

"Well," Shan said; "why not? Lead on, Brother!"

The jitter of anticipation eased somewhat. Val Con took a deep breath, nodded, and led the way across the rails.

Inside, the light was softer. The anticipation cooled to a mere flutter inside his head, which meant that he was close to . . . whatever. He hoped. Uncle Er Thom knew about the hunches, of course, but he didn't approve. Shan knew about them, too. It had been Shan who had come with him out in the rain when Merlin had gotten caught on a stepping stone in the stream, and would have drowned—or even been swept to the sea—and that had been a hunch. Well, Shan had trained with the Healers, after all, which Uncle Er Thom hadn't . . .

"Now where?" Shan asked.

Val Con moved his shoulders, and looked around them.

To their right was a transparent case, display lights striking sharp shards of light from rows of—blades. Knives were one of Val Con's hobbies; not only was he learning the art of the knife fight from his defense instructor, but he had made two small throwing blades of his own.

He took a step toward the case . . . another, and a third, which put his nose level with the top display row. Off his center by two degrees was a slim dagger in matte black, quiet among its flashier, bright-bladed cousins.

"Shan . . ." he said—

"Hey, you kids, get away from there!" a voice said in loud Terran.

Val Con jumped, startled, and bumped his nose against the glass.

"No weapons sales to anybody under twenty years, Standard," the voice continued, somewhat less loudly. "Pomerlooport rules." There was a small pause. "Your friend okay?"

"I believe so," Shan said. "Val Con?"

"I'm well," he managed, turning slowly, and resisting the urge to rub his nose. The person who had shouted was taller than Shan, dressed in a dusty dark sweater and baggy pants. He had a quantity of ginger hair standing on end, as if he, too, had more pressing things to do than bother with combs. His eyes were brown and very wide open.

"Either one of you got twenty Standards?" he asked, looking especially at Shan.

His brother smiled and shook his head. "Alas."

"No," Val Con admitted as the wide brown gaze moved to him. He cleared his throat. "I was . . . interested to see a Monix," he added.

The warehouseman—for he must be, mustn't he?—grunted softly. "Good eye, kid. That's a Monix, all right, an' a fair price on it, too. Problem being, like I said, I can't let you heft it to see if it suits your hand, much less sell it to you if it does. I do that, not only do I get hit with a stiff fine, you get arrested an' held 'til somebody old enough comes to pay *your* fine and take you back to your ship. Ain't fair, but that's how it is."

"I understand," Val Con said. "The law must be honored."

"That's the ticket," the man said, and looked back to Shan. "Interested in anything else?"

"Possibly. May we look about? We promise not to touch any weapons we may find."

"You find a weapon on the floor, you sing out," the warehouseman told him. "There ain't supposed to be any but what's in that case."

"Then my brother is safe from arrest," Shan said, smiling. He reached out and took Val Con's arm in a surprisingly firm grip.

A buzzer sounded from the rear of the warehouse, and the man turned toward it.

"Have fun," he said over his shoulder. "You break anything, you own it."

"Thank you," Shan said politely, "we'll be careful."

The man disappeared down an aisle barely wider than his shoulders. Shan released Val Con's arm and looked at him, eyebrows arched over light eyes.

"Was it the knife?" he asked, his voice low, speaking Liaden, now, rather than Terran.

" I. . .don't—" He paused, considering the jitter inside his head.

"No," he said. "But I don't know what it *is*."

"Do you know *where* it is?" Shan asked, patiently.

Val Con took a deep breath . . .

"I know that these things take time," Shan said after a moment. "However, we are exactly pressed for—"

"I know." Val Con looked about him, seeing the thin aisles overhung with boxes, cables uncoiling and drooping down like vines. "Shan, this is your time to trade. If this isn't promising—" It certainly didn't *look* promising . . .

"We can leave and I can carry you to the shuttle because you'll have a sick headache from not heeding your hunch," Shan finished. "That sounds like even less fun than being scolded by Father for wasting my time on port."

Val Con bit his lip, and spun on his heel. It seemed that there was a . . . very small . . . tug toward the center aisle. He walked that way, ducking beneath a cascade of tie-off filaments. Behind him, he heard Shan sigh, then the sound of his brother's footsteps.

They skirted two sealed plastic boxes that had fallen from a low shelf onto the floor, and the worker 'bot that was trying to put them back.

The aisle opened into a wide space, where a desk sat, drawers akimbo, papers fluttering in the breeze from a ceiling fan.

Drawn up to the desk like a chair was a packing crate; a flattened pillow on the side nearest the desk. Val Con felt something snap inside his head and he walked forward to kneel at the side of the crate.

It was slatted, not sealed tight, and between the slats he could see a solemn red blinking, like a low-power warning light.

He bent closer, intrigued, made out what looked like a battery array, and something else, that glimmered sullenly in the shadows.

He'd seen something like that—yes, signal-deadening wrap. He'd helped Shan and Master Ken Rik wrap some equipment they'd onloaded a couple ports back in muffles, not wishing to chance that even the sleeping signal might interfere with any of the *Passage's* live systems. There'd been a power light on that unit, too, but it had glowed a steady gold, indicating that the charge was strong.

"Val Con?" That was Shan, quietly.

He patted the crate. "This," he said, perhaps too loudly.

"Excellent," Shan said. "You'll be a subtle trader."

"I'm going to be a Scout," he said reflexively, and heard Shan sigh.

"What, exactly, *is* it?" he asked.

Val Con looked at the outside of the crate for a tag; found one almost at floor level, squinted at the faded words, and read them outloud.

"Environmental unit operations module with connectors."

He turned the tag over, found an ancient date and read outloud the rest of the information: "R. Spode Estate, Misc. Eqpt. Auction Lot 42."

Shan looked dubious.

"You're *certain*," he said.

Val Con nodded, and his brother sighed.

"All right, then. Stay here with it for a moment, will you? There was something in that aisle we just came down that I want a closer look at."

* * *

There had been a burst of brilliance, disorienting. Perhaps it was pain. In its wake came lethargy and a weakening of the will. Not sleep, this, but something more dire. He struggled against it, expending energy he ought best conserve, listening.

Listening for an answer.

No answer came.

He felt. . .movement, or perhaps it was his dying intelligence describing its last spiral. He sank, struggling. . .

Perhaps, indeed, he slept, for suddenly he wakened.

Wakened to a slow and steady trickle of energy. He sought the source, found the physical connection.

Humans wept at such moments. He—he swore an oath, whatever such things might mean in his diminished estate.

Whoever had come, whoever had heard, and heeded his call. That one he would serve, as well as he was able, for as long as he could.

* * *

Shan unsnapped three of the slats and Val Con skooched partway into the crate on his belly, jump-wire in hand. There was a bad moment when it seemed like the battery connection to the shrouded unit was frozen, but a bit of patient back-and-forth dislodged it. The jump-wire slid into the port and seated firmly. Val Con waited a long moment, chin resting on his folded arms, and sighed when the status light snapped over to orange.

"Meter shows juice flowing," Shan commented from outside the crate. "Rather more than a trickle."

"He's thirsty," Val Con said, dreamily, then shook himself out of the half-doze he'd fallen into. "I wonder if we ought to unwrap the main unit."

"We ought *not* to unwrap the main unit," Shan said firmly. "You do recall that we don't have the faintest notion what it actually is?"

"It's an environmental operations module," Val Con said.

"With connectors. Thank you. Do you see any sign of those connectors, by the way?"

Val Con looked around the cramped space. "I don't—no, wait. The slat directly opposite me is deeper than the one next."

"Oh, is it?"

There was the sound of purposeful footsteps and a flutter of light and shadow as Shan moved to the other side of the crate.

"I see it," he said, followed by the sharp snap of the slat being removed.

"Come out, Val Con, do," he added, and Val Con backed out of the crate on his elbows to join his brother at the workbench.

The low-power light had weighed in their decision to store the environmental module in one of the workrooms off of the cargo section. Also, now that it was his, Val Con was more than a little eager to see whatever it was he owned.

"They look like standard data-jacks," Shan said, laying them out on the bench.

Val Con picked up a black box about the size of his palm with whisker-wires bristling along one side.

"What do you suppose this is?"

Shan glanced at it. "Voice box."

"Of course," Val Con murmured.

"If you're satisfied for the moment," Shan said, "I suggest we lash the crate to the floor. Then, I will tend to my own cargo and you, if you'll allow me to express some brotherly concern, will get something to eat and perhaps a nap before Father returns."

It was a good plan—in fact, Val Con thought, as his stomach suddenly rumbled, it was an excellent plan. He said so, and the two of them made quick work of securing the crate. They left the workroom, walking together as far as the main cargo hall, where Val Con turned right, toward the ship's core and the crew cafeteria, and Shan went left, toward his small private cargo space.

* * *

He attempted to open one camera eye; enough to verify that the absorbent field was still in force—and closed it. The camera module worked, which was a grace given the years on it.

Now that there was energy available, and it having been so many years since an inventory had been done, he applied himself single-mindedly to that, thoroughly investigating every file and memory available to him. When that was done, he devised and solved logic problems, and designed airy confections of tri-spatial mathematics. The ability to plot trajectories, which he recalled as a primary function, was not immediately available to him. He supposed that Roderick Spode had removed the function, but had not cared to likewise remove his memory of it. Such minor cruelty matched his memory of the man.

He was doing his twelfth careful and complete inventory when something. . .changed.

It was subtle, not immediately definable, and scarcely had he noted it than it was driven from his attention by another, and not at all subtle, alteration in his condition.

He could . . . *hear*.

Small rustling sounds, that was what he heard, each one so precious that he shunted them immediately to core memory, attached to the recording of his astonished joy.

The rustling intensified, sharpening into static, which was interrupted by a heavy *thump*, and the mutter of—had that been a voice? A word?

Another *thump*, a crescendo of rustling, and—yes, it was a voice. And the word?

"Damn!"

Spoken with emotion, that word. But which emotion? Anger? Exultation? Disappointment? His own emotions were in a frenzy. By Deep Space Itself, he need to—

To see.

A scene swung into being before his newly opened eyes. A bench, on which he—or rather, whatever housed him at present—rested. Ahead, a wall of tools, some familiar, behind sealed transparent doors, an insulated utility apron and mitts hanging on the right.

To his right and rear, three crates of varying sizes were lashed to the floor. Directly behind him another crate was similarly lashed, and largely disassembled, half-obscured by a sheet of what was surely a signal-deadening wrap. To his immediate left—his liberator: unkempt dark hair, thin wrists overreaching the cuffs of a rumpled sweater, long fingers moving surely along the connections of what could be a voice-box.

"Where's the port, then?" The voice was soft; the words intelligible after the lexicon function sorted it. Liaden. That might be. . .unfortunate. And, yet—

"Yes!" Exultation was clear.

"Yes!" he echoed, his own exultation somewhat tempered by the cheap portable unit. The clever fingers tightened on the box, as the dark head turned toward him. Bright green eyes considered him seriously from behind tumbled bangs.

A child, he thought, amazed. His liberator was—a child.

"Are you all right?" another voice asked.

His eyes were tight-focused, he realized, and made the adjustment, zooming out until the entire small space was elucidated to him. The child had a companion—taller, white-haired. A parent, perhaps, or a parent's parent.

"Why shouldn't I be all right?" the child asked this taller companion, with perhaps a touch of impatience. "I've bumped my knee before."

"And I've dropped heavy objects on my thumb before," the companion retorted. "That doesn't mean it won't bruise, or doesn't hurt."

"I suppose," the child said dismissively, then suddenly turned more fully toward the other. "Your thumb isn't broken, is it, Shan?"

"No, it's not broken; only bruised. I've had worse doing cargo-shifting with Master Ken Rik. You hit that knee pretty sternly, however, and steel plate isn't the most forgiving surface."

"It's all right," the child said again.

"You should have let it fall," the taller one insisted.

"No, I couldn't have done that; suppose we'd broken it?"

"Whatever it is. Well. What else are we doing this shift, Brother? Or is liberating a so-called environmental unit from its muffle the awful whole?"

"I don't think," the child said slowly, looking down at the voice-box in his hand. "That is—it may not be an environmental unit."

"You amaze me. What might it be, then?"

"I don't know," the child confessed. "I researched the serial number in the manual archives, back a dozen-dozen years. Either the number was mis-transcribed . . ."

"Or it's contraband," the white-haired one said.

The child looked down at the box in his hand. There were slider controls along the side, which he manipulated.

"This isn't a very good voder," he said. "We ought to find better."

"We? This was your idea, as I recall it. What if it *is* contraband, Val Con?"

The child frowned. "I don't know. It was exactly this—whatever it is, as you say—that my . . . hunch led me to. I haven't been led to harm by a hunch before."

"Unless you count getting thoroughly soaked and scratched bloody."

"Merlin was frightened. And he likes to get wet even less than you do."

The white-haired—brother?—sighed.

"If there's anything else this shift, let's get to it, shall we? I'd like to get some sleep and you—"

"I only need to make a data connection," the child said rapidly. "The work of a moment. You go, Brother; I can do this."

"Certainly you can. I, however, will remain, as witness. Also, if Father decides to space you, I had rather be at your side, for how I would explain it to Mother, I have no idea."

The child laughed, a merry sound, and picked up a length of cable.

He looked at it hungrily. Data. Information. *Input*.

"If you don't mind sharing, what data are you connecting it to?"

"Since there is no manual, I follow standard protocols for re-servicing: Power, input, information," the child Val Con said, leaning close and making a connection in the unit that housed him with an audible snap. "As we said—it is possible that this is not an environmental unit at all, but . . . something other. That being so, I thought the best, broadest, and least perilous source of information is the ship's library."

His elder tipped his head, holding up a hand as the nether end of the cable approached the data-board.

"*Only* the ship's library."

"Yes."

"All right, then; have at it."

The child nodded, and seated the plug.

Had he been human, he would have drawn a breath.

Since he was not, he opened access to surface caches and allowed the data to flow.

* * *

A ripple disturbed the data-stream, momentarily disorienting, then forgotten, a shadow across the sun of input. His was hardly the only demand on the info circuits, after all, nor had he attempted to increase his access speeds or permissions, being a guest account. The library to which he had been given access was broad, but shallow. He understood that it was a popular library, well-stocked with fiction, history, biography, with a small holding of scholarly papers, and technical manuals.

Mathematics were there, of course, theory and programming, and he allowed himself moments to build and then rebuild a trajectory chart, wondering what Spode would have thought of that.

History, biography appended, went immediately into deep analysis, also the technical material. The scholarly papers required sorting, which he did, rapidly, appending them as appropriate to the larger analysis categories of history and technical. Fiction . . .

His impulse was to eliminate it—the storage capacity available to him was not so commodious that he could afford to waste space on whimsies. Yet, he hesitated, reluctant after so . . . very . . . long to relinquish any shred of data, no matter how trivial.

In the end, he cataloged the fiction, flicking through the texts as rapidly as he had once seen a man run his thumb down a deck of cards, riffling them to observe the face and orientation of each—and filed it in a mid-level cache.

That done, he set a sentinel to register the return of the child or his companion, and gave the greater part of his consciousness to analysis.

#

"Hello?"

The voice was recently familiar; its cadence rushed. The sentinel provided a match: The child had returned.

He opened his eyes to find the boy, frowning.

"Hello!" the child repeated sharply. "Are you in there?"

A direct appeal—and perhaps a trap. And, yet, the child had saved his life.

"I am," he replied, and stopped short of the fullness of what he had intended to say, horrified by the jagged sounds that came from the voice-box. Like shrapnel, his words, and nothing to inspire confidence in child or man.

The child's frown eased somewhat.

"It's a bad box, but the best we have. Quickly—you must tell me the truth—what data have you manipulated on this vessel?"

Manipulated? And the child asked for the truth.

"I have manipulated no data but that which has downloaded from the ship's library."

"In what way?"

"Sorting, analysis, cross-references."

The child held up a hand.

"That's too quick," he said, seriously. "It sounds like a lie—or that you haven't considered—when you answer so quickly. It's like—it's like bows. *I'm* too quick, and so I have to count when I bow, to keep proper time, so no one thinks that I'm mocking—or trying to frighten—them."

There was sense in what the child said.

"I understand," he said, and paused deliberately. "Tell me, what manipulation do you suspect I have performed?"

"Someone has tried to force the nav-comp and the main bank," Val Con said. "And I thought—you are not an environmental unit;

the serial numbers match nothing in any of our archives. Shan thinks you're a complex logic. I think you're a person. Are you?"

That was a leap. Fortunate or ill, it was a leap to a stable conception.

"I am, yes, a person."

The child bit his lip. "Uncle Er Thom—the attack came from this location. He will come here, or security will—"

"Young sir—" He paused, replaying his last hours of analysis and deep work. There had been—yes. He isolated the memory, froze it, and simultaneously locked it in core memory and moved a duplicate to an egress port.

"I have information," he said. "Is there an auxiliary unit to which I may transmit it?"

There was a snap; he expanded his awareness, saw the door open across the room, and a man stride through, a databox in one hand.

"Val Con, stand away." His voice was perfectly calm, and carried such a note of authority that it seemed there was no alternative but to obey.

The child, however, maintained his position, merely turning so that he faced the man.

"Uncle—he says that the attack was not his. I gave him access to the library—"

"Him?" Golden eyebrows rose. The man extended his free hand, imperious. "Come away, Val Con. Now."

The child shook his head. "Uncle—"

"I have," he said firmly, and as loudly as he was able, wishing he could hide the hideous knife-dance of his voice from his own perception; "information. May I transmit?"

The man moved, so quickly that it was a function of replay rather than real-time that captured him stepping forward, inserting himself between the child and what must be himself. He placed the data-box on the workbench, flipped three switches.

"Transmit at will," he said coolly.

He groped, found the ambient network, accessed the correct channel, and did as he was bid, keeping silent while the man accessed what had been sent.

A long moment passed. The man—Uncle—straightened and confronted him straightly.

"It's little enough," he said, his voice still cool, "and proves only what is already known. An attempted attack was launched from this location, utilizing the ambient network. As you are the only functioning logic in this space, I am forced to conclude that you were involved, whether you have been allowed to recall it or not."

That . . . produced terror. He had done inventory, but how could he know what had been introduced, to his detriment? He was a machine, Roderick Spode had repeatedly argued; the sum of his protocols and softwares. That it had been convenient for those who had caused his creation to have him self-aware was only that—convenience. Those who had made him could unmake him.

Or force him, unknowing and against his waking will, to work for the harm of children.

"If I have been complicit in such a thing, I hope that you will destroy me," he told the man. "I owe the child my life, and I will not repay that debt by endangering his."

Golden eyebrows rose over stern blue eyes.

"Now, that's well-said, and I like you for it. Which you intend, of course."

At that instant, it came again: a shadow over his perceptions, weighty now. Alert. *Malicious.*

He entered Command Prime, as effortlessly as if there had been no long sleep, no diminishing of his estate, between the last time and this.

One iteration of himself tracked the shadow in the ambient, while a second opened a new connection to the data-box and began transmission. A third opened access to the ship's library, followed it to the core, and crossed the firewalls into the main databank as easily as a child skipped over a stream.

"Uncle—"

Observed by a fourth instance of himself, the child placed his hand on the man's sleeve, his head tipped subtly to the right. He widened his range to encompass the crates to his right and rear. A match program snapped awake, shrilling alarm.

The configuration of those boxes had altered since the last time he had observed them.

Worse, the shadow overlay them, thickening in the ambient. He felt the coalescing of programs, of intent, and activated a fifth iteration of himself, which drilled through the deep files, rooting for command codes.

"I thought that I—that Shan and I—" the child continued. "That we might build Mother a butler. Certainly those at the reception were beautiful, and you'll recall that Master Trader Prael said they might be programmed to do anything . . ."

"Yes, I do recall that," the man said in his cool, calm voice, his eyes on the data-box and the storm building on the screen. He looked up and met the child's eyes.

"Val Con, I had asked you to stand away. This is your third warning. Leave the room. At once."

The child's lips parted; perhaps he meant to argue. He did not look away from his uncle's face, but he did swallow, take a breath, and, finally, bow his head.

"Yes, Uncle," he said humbly, and walked away.

Within the blue fog of the ambient, the shadow thrust, spitefully, at a cluster of code. He extended himself and blocked—the door slid properly open, allowing the child to exit.

"You also," Command Prime said, but the man shook his bright head.

"My ship," he said. "My children. My crew."

An order of protocol, and an imperative to defend. He understood such things, and honored them.

Honor was no defense, however, and defense the child's uncle surely required. The ambient fair trembled with spiteful intent, and power drenched the air.

The charge was still building. Discharged, it might not kill a man, though men were oddly fragile, but it would surely damage one. The man spun toward the sealed compartment, snatched it open and pulled out the utility apron.

The fifth iteration of himself, sent on the quest for codes, rejoined Command Prime, data unfolding like a flower.

The first iteration of himself met the menace in the ambient, codes a-bristle. The third, swimming aloof in the main banks, received those same codes and held them close.

The menace lunged—neither subtle nor clever, seeking to overcome him with a burst of senseless data laced with virus vectors. He shielded, and thrust past, to the intelligence behind the attack, certain that he would meet one such as himself.

So certain was he that he discounted the real threat, thinking it a mere device, belatedly recognizing the structure of the scantily shielded code.

Realizing his error, he made a recovery—a mere jamming of keys and code until the device fragmented and ceased functioning. It was ugly, brutal—and stupid. He ought to have merely captured, and subverted, it. Once, he could have done so.

Once, he would not have mistaken the actions of a simple machine intelligence for one of his own.

Inside the main banks, the third iteration of himself, armed with codes and an understanding of what he hunted, detected the device slipping down the data-stream, sparkling with malice. A data-bomb, much more coherent than that which had been hurled at him in the ambient.

This, he understood, as he subtly encompassed it, had been crafted well, and with intent. He halted the device, inserted the command keys, stripped out its imperative, plucked the rest of the construct apart, and absorbed the pieces, isolating them for later analysis.

Then, he pulled together the image scans he had stored, connecting them in a time plot: there the crated robot opening its own way into the workroom, there at the plug permitting highspeed data access, there rushing itself back and sealing the crate as voices in the hall had become the child Val Con.

Task done, the third iteration of himself rejoined Command Prime.

In the workroom, the man had not been idle. The disassembled pieces of the physical unit lay on the workbench, the man wearing the apron, a shielded spanner in one gloved hand.

He glanced to the data-box, where the whole of his actions were recorded, and at the images of the gifted danger, then directly *at him.*

"For your service to my ship, I thank you," he said. "What is your name?"

He paused, counting, mindful of the child's counsel. "I remember that I had a name," he said carefully. "I no longer recall what it was."

Golden brows lifted. "Age or error?"

"Design. I was decommissioned. It is my belief that I was to be destroyed. Erased."

"You are sentient." It was not a question, but he answered as if it were.

"Yes."

The man sighed and closed his eyes. "The child," he said, "is uncanny." His eyes opened. "Well.

"There will be tests, and conversations. Analysis. If it transpires that you are, after all a threat to Val Con's life, or to this ship, or any other, I will do as you asked me, and see you destroyed—cleanly and quickly."

That was just, though he still did not wish to die.

"And if I am found to be no danger to you or those who fall under your protection?" he asked.

The man smiled.

"Why, then, we shall see."

* * *

Thus it transpired that fiction assisted him, after all. For, after he had spoken at length with Er Thom yos'Galan, and with Scout Commander Ivdra sen'Lora, the first to ascertain the temper of his soul; the second to gain a certification of sentience, he agreed to hire himself as the butler at Trealla Fantrol, the house of yos'Galan on the planet Liad.

He studied—manuals, the records of one Ban Del pak'Ora, lists of alliances—and the works of a long-ago Terran.

In time, he signed a contract, and was presented, amidst much merriment to the mother of Val Con and Shan, the lifemate of Er Thom, who firstly, as Master Val Con had predicted, asked him his name.

"Jeeves, madam," he had said, pleased with the resonance and timbre the up-market voder lent his voice.

She laughed, the lady, and clapped her hands.

"Perfect," she said. "You'll fit right in."

The Space at Tinsori Light

Space is haunted.

Pilots know this; station masters and light keepers, too; though they seldom speak of it, even to each other. Why would they? Ghost or imagination; wyrd space or black hole, life—and space—is dangerous.

The usual rules apply.

* * *

Substance formed from the void. Walls rose, air flowed, floors heated.

A relay clicked.

In the control room, a screen glowed to life. The operator yawned, and reached to the instruments, long fingers illuminated by the wash of light.

On the screen—space, turbulent and strange.

The operator's touch on the board wakes more screens, subtle instruments. A tap brings a chronometer live in the bottom right of the primary screen. Beams are assigned to sweep near-space; energy levels are sampled, measured, compared.

The clock displays elapsed time: *293 units*.

The operator frowns, uncertain of what units the clock measures. She might have known, once. Two hundred ninety-three—that was a long phase. At the last alarm, it had shown 127 elapsed units; on the occasion before that, 63.

The operator turns back to her scans, hoping.

Hoping that it would prove to be *something* this time—something worthy of her. Of them.

The last alarm had been triggered by a pod of rock and ice traveling through the entanglement of forces that supported and enclosed them.

A rock pod. . .nothing for them.

She hadn't even had time for a cup of tea.

The alarm before the rock pod—had been nothing for them, either. Though they hadn't known that, at first.

They pulled it in, followed repair protocols, therapies, and subroutines. . .

She'd had more than a cup of tea, at least—whole meals, she'd eaten. She'd listened to music, read a book. . .But in the end there was nothing they could do, except take the salvage and ride the strange tide away again into that place where time, all unknown, elapsed.

The scans—*these scans*, now—they gave her rock, and mad fluctuations of energy. They gave her ice, and emptiness.

There ought to be something more. *Some*thing more, worthy or unworthy. The geometry of the space about them was delicate. The alarm would not sound for nothing.

The scans fluttered and flashed, elucidating a disturbance in the forces of this place. Breath-caught, the operator leans forward.

The scans detected, measured; verified mass, direction, symmetry. . .

The scans announced. . .

. . .a ship.

Any ship arriving here, was a ship in need.

The operator extended her hand and touched a plate set away from all the toggles, buttons, and tags that attended to her part of their function.

She touched the plate. And woke the Light.

* * *

This, thought Jen Sin yos'Phelium Clan Korval, *is going to be. . .tricky.*

Oh, the orders from his Delm were plain enough: Raise Delium, discreetly. Deliver the packet—there *was* a packet, and didn't he just not know what was in it. Discreet, the delivery, too. Of course. Delivery accomplished, he was to—discreetly—raise ship and get himself out of Sinan space, not to say range of their weapons.

Alive, preferably.

That last, that was his orders to himself, he being somewhat more interested in his continued good health and long-term survival than his delm. Package delivered was Korval's bottom line; the expense of delivery beyond her concern.

In any wise, the whole matter would have been much easier to accomplish, from discreet to alive, if Delium wasn't under active dispute.

Not that this was the riskiest mission he had undertaken at the Delm's Word during this late and ongoing season of foolishness with Clan Sinan and their allies. He was, Jen Sin knew, as one knows a fact, and without undue pride, Korval's best pilot. Jump pilot, of course, with the ring and the leather to prove it.

Of late, he would have rather been Korval's third or fourth best pilot, though that wouldn't have prevented him being plucked out from the Scouts, which had been clan and kin to him for more than half his life. No, it would have only meant that he would have served as decoy, to call attention away from Korval's Best, when there was a packet for delivery.

Well, the usual rules applied here, as elsewhere. If working without back-up: always know the way out, always carry an extra weapon, always know the state of your ship—and know that your ship is able and accessible—always be prepared to survive, and always remember that the Delm was Captain to the passengers. Being Korval's best pilot, his job was to fly where the passengers needed him to fly, at the direction of the Delm.

Jen Sin sighed. Gods knew he was no delm, and thankful for it, too. Delms did math in lives, set in courses that would be flown by pilots not yet born. The Delm decided who to spend, and when, for what profit to the clan. And just as well, Jen Sin acknowledged, that he wasn't clever enough to do those sorts of sums.

His attention was occupied for a bit, then, dodging various busy eyes in orbit, and when he had time to think again, at his ease between two security rings, he found he was thinking of his team.

When he'd first come out from the Scouts, he'd thought of them often—the comrades closer than kin; the six of them together stronger, smarter, faster than any one of them alone.

Well.

There was a time when he *could* have gone back, delm willing, which she hadn't been. Could have gone back, no questions asked, no accommodation required. *Could* have, then.

Now, what he had was *couldn't*, though *would* still burned in his belly, even now that it was too late. His team had long ago moved past their grief, taken on someone else, shifted tasks and priorities until they were, again, a team—different from the team it had been.

And no room for Jen Sin yos'Phelium, at all.

#

"I would prefer the Starlight Room, if it is available," he said, and passed over the identification for one Pan Rip sig'Alta, and a sixth-cantra, too.

The desk-man took both, bland-faced, scanned the card and returned it, the coin having been made to disappear.

"Sir, I regret. The Starlight Room is unavailable. May I suggest the Solar Wind?"

"The Solar Wind, excellent," he murmured, and received the key-card the man passed to him.

"The hallway to the right; the second door on your left hand. Please be at peace in our house."

That was scarcely likely—a certain tendency to unpeacefulness in perilous places being one of his numerous faults. Thus far, however, all was according to script. That, he told himself, firmly, was good.

Jen Sin entered the hallway, found the door, and used the key, stepping across the threshold immediately the door slid away, a man with no enemies, in need of an hour of solitude.

Two steps inside, the door already closed behind him, he checked—a man startled to find his solitary retreat already occupied.

This was also according to script—that there should be someone before him. Who, he had not been privileged to know. No matter, though—there were yet another few lines of code to exchange, which would in theory assure the orderly transfer of the packet tucked snug in an inner pocket of his jacket. And the safe departure of the courier.

Jen Sin allowed himself to display surprise before he bowed.

"Forgive me," he said to the severe young woman seated by the pleasant fire, a bottle of wine and two glasses on the table before her. "I had thought the room would be empty."

"Surely," said she, "the fault lies with the desk. However, it seems to me fortuitous, for I find myself in need of a companion other than my thoughts."

All and everything by the script. He ought to have been reassured. He told himself that.

Meanwhile, acting his assigned part, he inclined his head formally.

"I am pleased to accept the gift of comradeship," he murmured, and stepped toward the table with a Scout's silent footsteps.

He paused by the doubtless comfortable chair, the back of his neck feeling vulnerable. There remained one more matched exchange, to prove the case. Would the child never speak?

She looked up at him, and smiled, wistfully, so it seemed to him.

"Please," she said, "sit and share wine with me."

That. . .

. . .was *not* according to script, and now he saw it—the anomaly that his subconscious, ever-so-much cleverer than he, had noticed the moment he had cleared the threshold.

The wine bottle, there on the table between the two glasses. . .

Was uncorked.

Jen Sin kicked; the table, the glasses, the wine becoming airborne. He slapped the door open, heard glass shatter behind him, and a high scream of agony.

He did not look back as he stepped into the hall, turning left, away from the foyer where the doorman presided. Deliberately bringing to mind the floor plan he had memorized to while away the hours alone in transit to Delium, he ran.

Less than a half-minute later, he let himself out a service door, wincing as the alarm gave tongue. Then, he was again running at the top of his speed, down the delivery corridor to the street beyond.

#

He had not surrendered the packet, his ship, or his life, though he had pretended to give up the two latter.

The man hidden on the gantry, justifiably proud of the shot that had dropped him at the ship's very hatch, had taken the key from Jen Sin's broken fingers, turned, and slapped it home.

Obediently, the hatch rose. Jen Sin, slightly less dead than he had appeared, lurched to his feet, and broke the man's neck. The long rifle clattered to the landing pad, where he doubted it disturbed the gunman's three associates. The body he left where it fell, as he staggered into the lock, and brought the hatch down.

He crawled down the short hallway; dragged himself painfully into the pilot's chair. Gripped the edge of the board until his vision cleared. It hurt to breathe. Cunning thrust of the knife, there—he ought to remember it.

Time to go. He extended a hand, brought the board clumsily to life, his hands afire, no spare breath to curse, or to cry. The 'doc, that was his urgent need. He did know that.

Not yet, though. Not *just* yet.

He sounded a thirty-second warning, all that he dared, then gave *Lantis* her office, sagging in the chair, and not webbed in, and in just a while, a little while, only a while, a while. . . He shook his head, saw stars and lightning.

As soon as they gained Jump, it would be safe enough then, to tend his hurts.

An alarm screamed. He roused, saw the missile pursuing, initiated evasive action and clung to the board, to consciousness, in case his ship should need him.

So much for discretion, that was his thought, as *Lantis* bounced through lanes of orderly traffic, Control cursing him for a clanless outlaw, and not one word of sorrow for those firing surface-to-air into those same working lanes of traffic.

Korval either would or would not be pleased, though he had the packet. He kept reminding himself of that fact—he had the packet. The woman at the meeting room, spoke the lines out of order, no sense to it. If she were false, why not just finish the script and take what was not hers? If she were an ally, and captured—then, ah, yes, *then* one might well vary, as a warn-away—

She had not survived, he was certain of that, and to his list of error was added that he had cost Korval an ally. . .and added another death to his account. He might almost say, "innocent," save there were no innocents in this. He might, surely, say "dutiful," and even "courageous" might find a place in his report—and Korval—*he*—was in her debt.

His ship spoke to him. Orbit achieved. At least, he could still fly. He set himself to do so, heading for the up and out, the nearest Jump point, or failing that, the nearest likely bit of empty space from which he might initiate a Short Jump.

His side where the knife had gotten past the leather, that was bad; his fingers left red smears on the board. The doc. . .but *Lantis* needed him.

They had almost reached the Jump point, when a ship flashed into being so close the proximity alarms went off. Jen Sin swore weakly at pinheaded piloting, and a moment later discovered that not to be the case at all.

The new ship fired; the beam struck directly over the engines.

The shields deflected it, and there came evasive action from the automatics, but the other ship was a gunboat, no slim and underarmed courier.

The Jump point was that close. Once in Jump space, he would have some relief. Enough relief that he might live through this adventure.

There really was no other choice; he had no more time on account.

Blood dripped from fingers remarkably steady as they moved across the board, diverting everything but the minimum amount necessary to function—from life support, from auxiliary power.

From the shields.

He fed everything to the engines, and *ran* for the Jump point, as if there were no gunboats within the sector, much less the ship that even now was launching enough missiles to cripple a warship.

They hit the point with too much velocity, too much spin; in the midst of an evade that had no chance of succeeding. He greatly feared that they brought the missile with them.

Jen Sin groped for and hit the emergency auto-coords, felt the ship shiver, saw the screens go grey—

And fainted where he sat.

* * *

The Light pulled and riffled the files from the ship. The operator kept one eye on its screen while she pursued her own sort of data.

Engine power was minimal, and life support also; the shields were in tatters. The dorsal side showed a long, deep score, like that delivered from an energy cannon. That the hull had not taken worse damage—that was something to wonder at. Still, her readings indicated life support and other services low past the point of danger.

It was, the operator acknowledged, a ship in dire trouble, yet it held air, it held together, and it had come under its own power into the space at Tinsori Light. All those things recommended it, and the operator felt a cautious thrill of anticipation.

If the ship were fit to be repaired—but that was for the Light to decide.

If the pilot lived—her duty fell there.

The operator shivered, in mingled anticipation, and fear.

* * *

They'd taken bad hits, him and his ship, and unless they raised a repair yard, or a friendly station soon, there was no saying that they'd either one survive.

He'd come to in Jump with emergency bells going off and a blood-smeared board lit yellow and red. It took determination, and a couple of rest periods with his forehead pressed against the board while pain shuddered through him, and his sluggish heartbeat filled his ears—but he pulled the damage reports.

Whatever had hit them as they entered Jump had been—*should have been*—enough to finish them. The main engine was out; the hull was scored, and there was a slow leak somewhere; life support was ranging critical and running off impulse power, along with the lights and screens.

In short, he was a pilot in distress and with a limited number of choices available to him.

One—he could manually end Jump and hope *Lantis* held together, that they would manifest in a friendlier portion of space than the port they had just quit, and within hailing distance of, if not an ally, at least a neutral party.

Two—he could ride Jump out to its natural conclusion. Normal re-entry would be kinder to his ship's injuries. His own injuries. . .

He looked down at his sticky hands, the Jump pilot's ring covered with gore, and allowed himself to form the thought. . .

I am not going to survive this.

Oh, he could—probably—crawl across the cabin and get himself into the autodoc. But under emergency power, the 'doc would only stabilize him, and place him into a kindly sleep until such time as ship conditions improved.

He may have blacked out again, just there. Certainly it was possible. What roused him was. . .was.

Ah.

Lantis had exited Jump. They were. . .someplace.

Gasping, he leaned toward the board, squinting at screens grown nearly too dark to see.

The coords meant nothing to him. He remembered—he remembered hitting the auto-coords. But the auto-coords were for Korval safe spots—the ship yard, the Rock; quiet places located in odd corners of space, such as might be discovered by Scouts and pilots mad for knowing *what was there*? Auto-coords had taken stock of *Lantis* as injured and hurt as it was, and, measured through some prior delm-and-pilot's priorities, cast them together through limitless space to one particularly appropriate destination, to one last hope.

He looked again at screens and arrival data. The coords still meant nothing to him, though their absolute anonymity to a pilot of his experience and understanding gave him to believe that pursuit was now the least of his problems.

The space outside his screens was a place of pink and blue dusts pirouetting against a void in which stars were a distant promise.

If there was a friend of Korval in this place, it would, he thought, be good if they arrived. . .soon.

As if his thought had called the action, an interior screen came to life. Someone was accessing the ship's public files.

Hope bloomed, so painful and sudden that he realized he had, indeed, given up himself and his ship. There was someone out there—perhaps a friend. Someone who cared enough that it did them the honor of wanting to know who they were.

Jen Sin reached to the board, teeth gritted against the pain, and did pilot's duty, waking the scans and the screens, directing the comp to pull what files might be on offer at the address helpfully provided by their interrogator.

He found the visual as the files scrolled onto the screen—stared at both in disbelief, wondering if everything, from his waking at Jump-end to this moment, were nothing other than the final mad dreams of a dying mind.

A station rose out of the dust, like no station he had ever seen, all crags, sharp edges, and cliffs. There were no visible docking bays, nor any outrigger yards. From the center of the uncompromising angularity of it, rose a tower; white light pulsed from its apex in a rhythm of six-three-two.

On the screen, the information: *Welcome to Tinsori Light, Repairs and Lodging.*

He touched the query button, but no further information was forthcoming.

An alert trilled, and Jen Sin blinked at the stats screen even as he felt the beam lock around *Lantis*.

For good or for ill, friend or foe, Tinsori Light was towing them in.

* * *

The pilot had queried the Light.

The pilot was *alive.*

The operator rose, hands automatically smoothing her robe. Once, she thought, she must have had a robe that wrinkled, showed wear, became stained. This garment she wore now, here, in this role—this robe was never mussed, or rumpled. Always, it was fresh, no matter how long she wore it, or how much time had elapsed.

But the pilot—alive. She stared at the screen, as if she could see through the damaged hull, into the piloting tower, and the one sitting conn. Was the pilot wounded? she wondered. It seemed likely, with the ship bearing such injuries.

Wounded or whole, there were protocols to be followed, to insure the pilot's safety, and her own. The Light would have its sample—that she could not prevent. Though, if the pilot were wounded, she thought suddenly, that might go easier; there would be no resistance to entering the unit.

The Light was not always careful of life. That the pilot might be frail would not weigh with it. It was hers, to shield the pilot, to follow the protocols, and to insert herself between the Light and the pilot, should it come to be necessary.

She looked again to her screens, at the progress of the ship toward the service bay.

Should she, she wondered suddenly, *contact* this pilot? If she was injured, she might want reassurance, and to know that assistance was to hand.

The operator studied the screens; the lines of the ship being towed into the repair bay.

She sighed.

It was *like* a design she knew. The Light obviously considered it like enough that repairs could be made. But languages were not so easy as ships.

In the end, the operator tucked her hands into the sleeves of her robe, watching until the ship entered the repair bay.

* * *

Blackness ebbed.

He observed its fading from a point somewhat distant, his interest at once engaged, and detached. First the edges thinned, black fogging into grey, the fog continuing to boil away until quite suddenly it froze into a crystalline mosaic, the whole glowing with a light so chill he shivered in his distant point of observation.

In that moment, he became aware of himself once more; aware that he was alive, healed, perhaps returned to perfect health.

The chill light sharpened, and from it came. . .nothing so gross as a whisper. *A suggestion.*

A choice.

He *had* been returned to optimal functioning; to perfect health. But there existed opportunity. He might become *more* perfect. His abilities might be enhanced beyond the arbitrary limits set upon him by mortal flesh. He might be made stronger, faster; he might sculpt the minds of others, turn enemies to allies with a thought; bend event to favor him—all this, and more.

If he wished.

The decision-point was here and now: Remain mortally perfect, and perfectly limited. Or embrace greatness, and be more than ever he had—

A sharp snap, and the complaint of pneumatic hinges shattered the crystal clarity of the voice. Warm air scented with ginger wafted over naked skin.

Jen Sin yos'Phelium opened his eyes. Above him, a smooth hood, very like to an autodoc's hood. To his left, a wall, supporting those hinges. To his right, the edge of the pad he lay upon, and a space—dull metal walls, dull metal floor, and, nearby, a metal chair, with what was perhaps a robe draped across its back and seat.

He took a deep and careful breath, tears rising to his eyes at the sweet, painless function of his lungs. He tasted ginger on the back of his tongue—knowing it for a stimulant. She'd gotten him to the 'doc after all.

That thought gave pause. He closed his eyes again, taxing his memory.

There had been a woman—had he dreamed this? A woman with a pale pointed face, her black eyes large and up-slanted, and a hood pulled up to hide her hair. She had picked him up—surely, *that* was a true memory! Picked him up, murmuring in some soft, guttural tongue that was almost—almost—one that he knew...

And there; a key phrase or sound, a match in a part of his memory he was sure was as new as his health.

"Do you wish to sleep, a better bed awaits you," a voice commented. The voice of his rescuer. Now that his brain was clear, he understood her perfectly well, though she spoke neither Liaden nor Trade, nor the Yxtrang language, either, though closer to that tongue than the other two. Sleep-learned or not, it was a language his Scout-learning marveled at even as he heard it.

He opened his eyes and beheld her, standing quite in plain sight next to the chair. Wordlessly, she lifted the robe, shook it, and held it wide between two long, elegant hands.

"My thanks." He rolled off of the mat, expecting the shock of cold metal against his soles; pleased to find that the floor was warmed. The robe, he took from her hands and slipped on, sealing the front, and leaving the hood to hang behind.

That done, he bowed, deeply, giving all honor to one who had saved his life.

"I am Jen Sin yos'Phelium Clan Korval," he said. "My name is yours, to use at need."

"There is scarcely any need of names here," his companion said, coolly amused. "Keep yours; it will profit you more."

"Will it?" He straightened and looked at her.

She was taller than he, the starry robe hiding the shape of her. Her face was as he remembered, pointed, pale, and solemn; the hood was cast back, revealing tumbled curls of some color between yellow and white. Relieved of the burden of his garment, she had tucked her hands into the sleeves of her robe.

"I wonder if I may know your name," he said.

"It is possible that you may know it," she answered. "If you do, you might tell it me. It would be pleasant to hear, and to remember from time to time, though as I said, there is little use for such things as names, here."

He cast her a sharp glance, but she seemed serious, and there was the language interface; this near-Yxtrang tongue had an ambiguous question protocol.

That being so, he moved a shoulder in regret.

"I have said the thing badly," he admitted. "What I had wished was to learn your name, or what you are called by your comrades, or yourself."

"Oh." It seemed that she was disappointed, and he was, foolishly, regretful, that he had no name to bestow upon her. "I am the Keeper of the Light at Tinsori. Others before you have chosen to address me as Keeper. It is enough of a name, I suppose."

He bowed gently. "Light Keeper, I am in your debt."

"I do my duty. There is no occasion for debt."

"And yet, I place a value upon my life. That you return it to me—that is not without value. My ship—"

She raised a hand. "Your ship is under repair. Our facilities here are. . .old, and perhaps non-standard. However, with some small modification, your ship can be brought back to functionality. The Light proceeds with that work."

"Is there an estimate for completion?" he asked.

She frowned. "No."

That made him uneasy, but he merely inclined his head. "It is true that such damage as *Lantis* sustained might require some time to repair. I regret that I must ask—"

"Ask what you might," she interrupted, brusquely. "I am not so accustomed to company that I will naturally realize what you wish to know."

"To give a Scout permission to ask questions is generous beyond sense," he said, attempting lightness. "Immediately, I take advantage, and ask if there is a pinbeam unit on-station."

She tipped her head, and he saw the glint of what might have been drops of crystal in the tumble of her curls.

"There is not," she said.

That was disappointing, but not necessarily fatal.

"I then ask—may I gain access to my ship, which has such a unit. If I may draw power from the station, the message might be sent." He added, as gently as he might. "I mean only to let my delm know that I am well. This is no ploy to call enemies down upon you."

She laughed at that, which was as startling as it was engaging. No sooner had the sound faded then he wanted her to laugh again.

"To call enemies down on Tinsori Light! That has been done. It did not go well for them." She slipped her hands out of her sleeves and smoothed the front of her robe.

"Look you, Jen Sin yos'Phelium Clan Korval—messages do not travel outward from Tinsori Light; and in all the time that has elapsed since our founding, no message has ever reached us from elsewhere. The space. . .does not behave as normal space must do. Worse, even the attempted transmission of such a message might disturb the balances that keep us here, and now. I cannot allow it. The Light, I fear, *will also* not allow it."

He took that as his answer, for now, and assayed another question.

"May I know where my clothes are? There was something. . .dear in my jacket, and I would not see it lost."

"I have placed your possessions in your quarters," she said. "Do you want to go there now?"

His quarters, was it? And no time estimated for the completion of repairs, nor access to a pinbeam. It began to seem as if he were a prisoner, more than a customer, but until he knew more of this place, he dare not do anything but bow his head and murmur.

"I would very much like to see my quarters, thank you."

#

He had expected standard station accommodations—which was to say, slightly smaller than his quarters aboard *Lantis*. Instead, he was shown to a room very nearly the size of the apartment he so seldom rested in, at Jelaza Kazone. The metal walls had been softened with hangings, and the floor had been spread with rugs. Pillows and coverlets in bright colors covered the bed. There was a screen mounted in such a way that it could be easily seen from the bed, and a small carved chest on which the contents of his pockets had been scrupulously placed.

Leaving his host by the door, Jen Sin approached the chest—cantra pieces and lesser coins; a flip-knife of Scout issue; his snub-nosed hideaway; a leather-rolled tool kit; and the green-wrapped packet, its ribbons and seals undisturbed, though displaying a few distressing stains upon its surface.

"The leathers are being repaired," she said in her abrupt way. "There are robes a-plenty."

"I thank you," he murmured and turned, holding up his hand. "I had been wearing a ring. . ."

"Yes." She tucked her hands into her sleeves and came like a wraith across the rug-strewn floor. She was well within kin-space when she finally stopped her advance, and he using all a Scout's discipline to stand easy where he stood.

She slipped her right hand out of her sleeve and extended it, fingers curled. He held out his hand, and felt the cold heaviness of it strike his palm. A downward glance told him it was his own ring, sparkling as if it were new-made.

"I cleaned it," she said.

"And I thank you for that kindness as well," he said sincerely, remembering the gore-encrusted stones. "A third time, I am in your debt."

"No," she said.

"But I stand at a disadvantage," he protested. "Is there nothing that I might do for you, to balance us?"

The black eyes lifted to his face.

"I wonder," she said slowly, "if you play cards."

#

The deck had been strange to him; the game stranger, though he had the rules to an hundred card games committed to memory.

The Light Keeper played with an intensity that was somewhat alarming, and when they paused the play for a meal—the most basic of yeast-based rations—she ate with that same intensity, as one starved for sensation.

After the meal, he pronounced himself weary—which fell short of being a complete falsehood—and she obligingly led him back to his room, standing aside while he entered, the door closing behind him.

Panic took him in the instant he heard the door seal, and he spun, threw himself at the blank wall—and all but stumbled out into the hallway, and the Keeper's arms.

She frowned.

"Are you not tired, after all?"

"I had wanted to see if it opened for me," he said. "The door."

"That's wise," she answered gravely, and left him there, vanishing 'round the corner of the hall.

He stood for perhaps two dozen heartbeats after she was gone, feeling foolish. Then he turned and re-entered his room.

#

They fell into a schedule of sorts. The Light Keeper had duties that held her at odd hours, during which time Jen Sin partook of the station's library. When the Light Keeper's duty permitted, they walked together, she showing him somewhat of the station.

It was a strange place, the station, and it seemed that he and the Light Keeper were the only persons who walked its halls. He inquired after other travelers, traders, or those in need, but his guide only said that there was very little traffic in the space about Tinsori.

Moreover, the station contained such amusements as were strange to him. One room she led him to simulated planetary weather, so that they were rained upon, dried by a warm wind and then snowed on. The Light Keeper laughed, and spun, shaking her crystal-beaded curls, her robe flaring out to show naked long toes and trim pale ankles.

Jen Sin caught her arm and pulled her out into the warmer hall.

"Is it not delightful?" she asked.

"Truth said, it casts me off-balance," he answered, trying unsuccessfully to dry his face with a snow-spangled sleeve. "Weather changes on-planet come with warnings, to simply have random weather flung at one—it distresses me."

He was likewise distressed by the room that produced odors in an indiscriminate aural medley, though the green room found his favor—flowers and vegetables alike.

"Here, this one is ripe," he said, touching the round red cheek of a tomato. "Shall we take it back with us for the evening meal?" This was his third day on the station, and he was growing tired of yeast.

The Light Keeper frowned at him. "Eat a plant?"

"A vegetable, but yes. Why not?"

"I never thought of it," she said.

"Someone must have done," he said lightly, plucking the fruit. "Most stations have hydroponic sections, so residents may reap the benefit of fresh food. Yeast alone does not satisfy all one's appetite." He smiled at her. "I would have thought that one as open to sensation as yourself would have sampled every leaf here."

"Truly, it did not occur," she said, and he could see that she was troubled. "How. . .odd. I must have forgotten."

They exited the garden and continued their walk.

"What duty are you called to," he asked her, "in the control room?"

He thought for a moment she would not answer him, and indeed, it was impertinence, to ask. But his browsing of the library, of those volumes written in a language he could read, had begun to fill him with unease.

The Light Keeper shrugged. "I prevent the Light from doing mischief," she said. "And keep it to its location."

It was his moment to frown.

"The station drifts?"

"No," she said. "The station moves of its own volition, within the constraints of coords that balance with the expanding edge of things. Part of my function is to keep us at that expanding edge, to maintain the energy levels that keep the coords constant. The Light would be better pleased, if we were closer in, where it could wield its influence."

"Influence," he repeated, as they came to a place where the corridor split. Unthinking, he turned right—and stopped immediately when she caught his sleeve.

"Not that way."

"Why not?"

A hesitation. "Old damage. The hall is not safe."

"May I assist? I am a Scout, and have strange abilities of my own."

She looked doubtful. "If you like, I will open the schematics to you."

Oh, would she, indeed? Jen Sin bowed softly.

"I would like that very much, indeed."

#

The Light Keeper ate her half of the fruit greedily, then grilled him on what else out of the garden section might be edible. He laughed and threw his hands up, palms out, to fend her eagerness.

"Come, if you will open the schematics, then open the garden records, as well, and I will apply myself to research."

"Done!"

He laughed again, lowering his hands.

"I see I have my work in line."

"You asked for work," she pointed out in her practical way.

"So I did."

She tipped her head. "Jen Sin, I wonder if you might do something. . .else for me."

He looked into her tip-tilted black eyes, and thought he knew what she might ask. Indeed, he was surprised that she had not asked before, as sense-starved and solitary as she was.

"I will do anything that is in my power," he told her gently.

#

"What are these?" he asked, later, fingering the crystal drops in her hair.

"My memories," she said drowsily, her head on his shoulder.

He was drowsy himself, but a Scout fails of asking questions when he is dead.

"If you brush them out, will you forget yourself?"

"No. But if something happens and I am not wearing them, I will have no prompts and the Light will be unwatched."

Perhaps that made sense in some way, but he lacked context. He would have pressed her, but her breathing told him that she had slipped into sleep.

He sighed, nestled his chin against her curls, and followed.

* * *

"What progress," she asked the Light, "on the repairs?"

Progress, came the reply.

The Keeper bit her lip.

"When will repairs be complete?" she asked.

Unknown.

This mode was unfortunate. It was behavior from a distant time, when the Light had first come into the care of the Sanderat. The Keeper closed her eyes, called up her will, thrust it at the Light.

"You will tell me when repairs will be complete and when Jen Sin yos'Phelium Clan Korval may depart, to continue his lawful business."

Are you ready to be alone again? The pilot amuses you, does he not? What harm to keep him?

Yes, this was very bad, indeed. The Light was at its most dangerous when it offered your heart's desire. She breathed deeply, and made her will adamantine.

"I will have a time when the ship in your care will be repaired and able. The pilot is his own person; he has duty. It is our duty to assist him, not disrupt him."

It is your duty to assist.

"It is, and as you serve me, it is your duty, also."

There was a silence. Rather a lengthy silence.

The ship will be able to depart in six station days.

So soon? She bowed her head.

"That is well, then. Keep me informed."

* * *

The schematics were fascinating—and horrifying.

Jen Sin had been a member of a Scout Exploratory Team. He, as all explorer Scouts, had been well-drilled on the seeming and the dangers of what was called Old Tech. His team had discovered a small cache of what might have been toys—small, crude ceramic shapes that might infiltrate a man's mind, make him receptive to thoughts that he would not recognize as belonging to an Other.

The cache of toys they had found had been depleted, being able to effect nothing more than a sense of melancholy and foreboding in those unheedful enough to pick them up. His team—well. Krechin had wrapped them in muffle, and sealed them into a stasis box until they could be properly handed over to the Office of Old Technology, at Headquarters.

The toys had been frightening enough, but he had an extra burden of knowledge, for he had read the logs and diaries of Clan Korval, as far back as Cantra yos'Phelium, who had brought the understanding that the old universe and the old technologies had together been the downfall of vast civilizations. And that had been old technology in small gulps, as might be found in a toy, or a personalized hand-weapon, or a geegaw worn for nefarious purpose.

To find a working, *aware* structure entirely built from forbidden tech—that was enough to give a Scout nightmares. Even Korval might quail before such a thing.

And the Light Keeper's purpose was to keep it from *doing mischief*?

Mischief, by the gods. And his ship was in its keeping. Worse. His ship was in *its power*, being modified, never doubt it, as he stood by—and did nothing.

Jen Sin closed the schematics and rose from the desk. He quit the library, and walked toward the hub, where there was a gym.

Exercise would calm him.

And then he would need to speak with the Light Keeper.

#

"Tell me," he said to the Light Keeper, as she settled her cheek on his shoulder, "about this place."

She stirred, eyelashes fluttering against his skin.

"This space?"

"No, the station," he murmured. "The schematics woke questions."

She laughed softly. "What sorts of questions, now?"

"Well. How did the station come to be? Who built it? How did you come to keep it? Where are the others? . . .Those sorts of questions. I don't doubt I can find more, if you wish."

"No, those will do, I think."

She sighed, relaxing against him so completely that he thought for a moment that he had been cheated, and she had slipped over into sleep.

"How the station came to be. My sisters of the Sandaret believed that the Great Enemy built it. We found it abandoned, and riding in space where a waystation had been sore needed. The Soldiers were in favor of destroying it, but it was in Sandaret space, and we undertook to Keep it.

"Three of our order were dispatched. . .Faren, Jeneet, and. . .Lorith."

She tensed. He held his breath.

"Lorith," she breathed. "That is *my* name."

"May I address you thus?" he asked, when several minutes had passed and she had said nothing more, nor relaxed.

"Yes." She sighed again, and became. . .somewhat. . .less tense.

"What happened," he murmured, "to Faren and Jeneet?"

"Faren died in the storm," she whispered. "We were without power, adrift, for many elapsed units. When we came to rest, and repairs were made—it was no longer possible to reclaim her. The Light took new samples, from Jeneet, from me."

Samples. He repressed the shiver, sternly, and asked his next question softly, "What storm was that, Lorith?"

"Why, the big storm, that shifted everything away from where it had been. When it was done, the Light was. . .where you found it, and not in orbit about Tinsori, as it had been. Tinsori, we were not able to locate. The coordinates of our present location. . .were not possible. Jeneet took our boat and went out to find where we were. That was. . .Much time has elapsed, since then. I fear that she has been lost, or died, or taken up in battle."

Korval had an odd history; it was odder still to hear that history from other lips, from another perspective, and yet, *that* war, that had displaced a universe or more. . .from one space-time to another.

That war had ended hundreds of years ago.

He stroked her hair, feeling the crystal beads slide through his fingers.

"Lorith," he said, gently, oh, so very gently. "I cannot allow my ship to rest any longer in care of the Light."

She raised her head and looked down at him, eyes wide and very black.

"It said. . .six days, as we measure them here, when time is aware. Six days, and your ship will be ready." She frowned. "I have exerted my will. You will come to no harm, though I will. . .miss you."

"You need not. Come with me."

"No, who would Keep the Light? It might do anything, left to itself."

So it might.

He sat up, and she did, drawing a crimson cover over her naked shoulders.

"I must go," he said, and slid out of bed, reaching for his leathers.

* * *

He was determined and she could not—would not—influence him to wait. She showed him the way to the repair bay, hearing the voice of the Light.

Little man, you will have your ship when it is properly prepared.

Jen Sin checked, then continued toward the place where the tunnel intersected the hall.

"The pilot decides when his ship is ready," he said aloud. "I go now, and I thank you, and the Light Keeper, for your care."

She hardened her will, and pushed at the Light.

"Let him go to his duty," she said, and added, terrified for his safety, "Unless the ship is not functional."

She was an idiot; her fear for him softened her will. And in that moment, the Light struck.

The walls crackled; she felt the charge build, and simultaneously threw her will and herself between Jen Sin and the bolt.

She heard him scream, her name it was—and then heard nothing more.

* * *

He came to himself in the library, with no memory of having arrived there. He supposed that he had run—run like a hare from Lorith's murder, to save his own precious self, to *survive* against every odd—*that* was Korval's talent.

Craven, he told himself, running his hands into his hair and bending his head. He was weeping, at least he had that much heart.

But the Scout mind would not be stilled, and too soon it came to him that—he dared not leave the Light unwatched. For who knew what it might do, left alone?

He had the schematics, and his Scout-trained talents. Did he dare move against it and risk his life? Or ought he to stand guard and prevent it doing harm?

"Jen Sin?" He would swear that he felt her hand on his hair, her voice edged with concern. "Were you hurt?"

Slowly, he lifted his face, staring into hers, the pointed chin, the space-black eyes, and the crystal beads glittering in pale, curly hair.

"You were killed," he said, toneless.

She stepped away. "No."

"Yes!" He snapped to his feet, the chair clattering backward, snatched her shoulders and shook her.

A thought tantalized, then crystallized.

"*How many times* has it killed you?"

"I don't know," she said, shockingly calm. "Perhaps I die every time we drift back to quiet after an alert, and the Light remakes me at need. Does it matter? I am always myself, and I have my memories. The sample, you know."

He stared, speechless, feeling her fragile and real under his fingers.

"The sample, of course," he agreed. "What came of Jeneet's sample, Lorith?"

"She did not use the beads, and when I called her back, she remembered nothing."

He closed his eyes briefly, recalling the unit he had risen from, and the crystal-cold voice, offering him a choice.

"Jen Sin?"

He raised his hand and ran his fingers through her hair, feeling the cool beads slip past his skin.

"I wonder," he said, softly. "Is there a. . .sample of me?"

Her eyes flickered.

"Yes."

"And have you more beads?"

"Yes."

"Then this is what I think we should do, while I wait for my ship to be...properly prepared."

* * *

The operator sat at her board, and watched the ship tumble out of the repair bay. The scans elucidated a vessel in good repair, the hull intact, all systems green and vigorous.

She took a breath, and watched her screens, dry-eyed, until the Jump-glare faded, and the space at Tinsori Light was empty, for as far as her instruments could scan.

* * *

He brought the pinbeam online, entered the message, in Korval House code. The message that would warn the clan away, and see Tinsori Light scrubbed from the list of auto-coords in Korval courier ships. The message that would tell the delm the Jump Pilot's ring was lost, along with the good ship and pilot. The message that would tell the delm that when she needed another packet delivered, it could never again be Jen Sin who would do it.

Emergency repairs at Tinsori Light. Left my ring in earnest. The keeper's a cantra-grubbing pirate, but the ship should hold air to Lytaxin. Send one of ours and eight cantra to redeem my pledge. Send them armed. In fact send two...

The 'beam went. He waited, patiently, for the ack, looking down at his hands, folded on the board, ringless and calm.

He reviewed his plan, and found it, if not good, certainly necessary.

A ship *properly prepared* by an agent of the Great Enemy? How could he bring such a ship into the galaxy proper, save for one thing only?

Comm chimed; the 'beam had been acknowledged by the first relay.

* * *

She felt a hand settle on her shoulder, and looked up, finding his reflection in a darkened screen.

"He's gone?"

"Yes."

She spun the chair and came to her feet; he dropped back to give her room, the beads glittering like rain in his dark hair.

"Now, it is for us," she said. "Will we survive it?"

He smiled and held out his hand, the big ring sparkling on his finger.

"Many times, perhaps," he said.

* * *

Space is haunted.

Pilots know this; station masters and light keepers, too; though they seldom speak of it, even to each other. Why would they? Ghost or imagination; wyrd space or black hole, life—and space—is dangerous.

The usual rules apply.

About the Authors

Sharon Lee and Steve Miller are the authors of eighteen collaborative novels of science fiction and fantasy, most set in the Liaden Universe® a space opera geography of their own devising. Their latest novel is Ghost Ship, published by Baen Books in August 2011. Dragon Ship is coming from Baen, in September 2012.

In addition to her work in the Liaden Universe® Sharon has also seen published a contemporary fantasy, Carousel Tides, and two mysteries set in the town of Wimsy, Maine.

For a more-or-less-complete bibliography, as well as bios, and a list of upcoming author appearances, please drop by http://www.korval.com

Thank you

for your interest in
and support of
our work
Sharon Lee and Steve Miller